Gillfillan
1986
Eugene Kraus

HEARTS

Hearts

THOMAS R. NASSISI
and
ARLENE DUBANEVICH

MACMILLAN PUBLISHING CO., INC.
NEW YORK

Copyright © 1981 by Thomas R. Nassisi and Arlene Dubanevich

Macmillan Publishing Co., Inc.
866 Third Avenue, New York, N.Y. 10022
Collier Macmillan Canada, Ltd.

Library of Congress Cataloging in Publication Data
Main entry under title:
Hearts.
1. Heart—Caricatures and cartoons. 2. Wit
and humor, Pictorial. 3. Heart—Anecdotes, facetiae,
satire, etc. I. Nassisi, Thomas R. II. Dubanevich,
Arlene.
NC1763.H38H4   741.5′9   81-8161
ISBN 0-02-588340-2   AACR2

10   9   8   7   6   5   4   3   2   1

Printed in the United States of America

To my parents, silly Sophie and smiling Frank,
and
to my husband, joking J.

Thanks to J., Libby, Lila, Marion, and Tom.
Special thanks to Sandy.

miles & miles of heart

heart to heart

heart massage

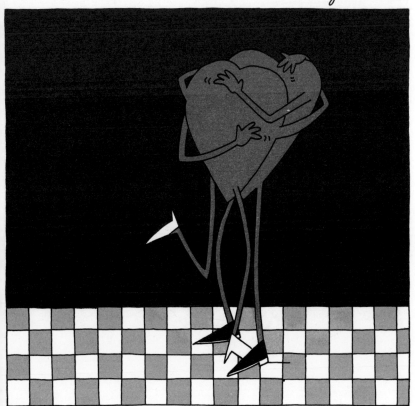

open heart

change of heart

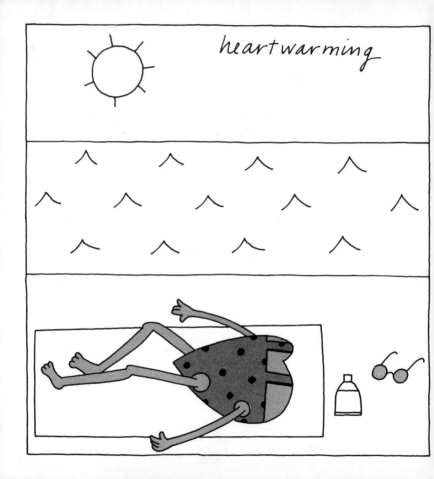

heart surgeon

with a
heavy heart

heart transplant

hearts & flowers

hearts all aflutter

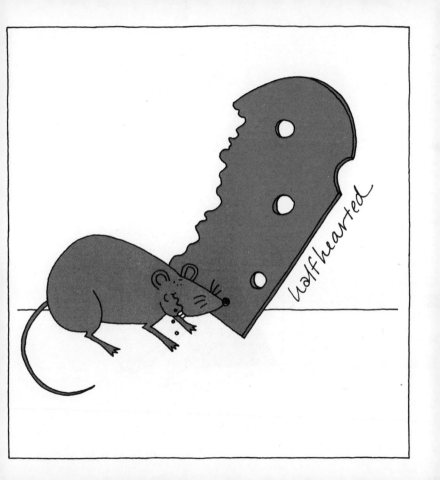

heartstrings

learn by heart

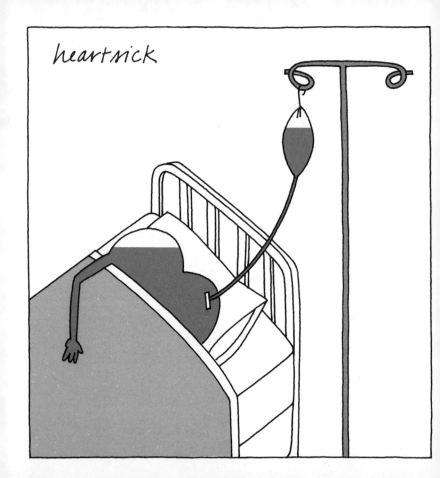

cross my heart

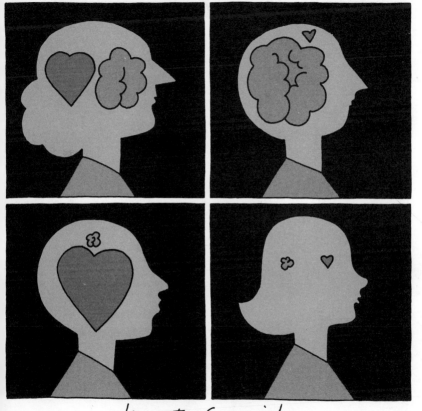

hearts & minds

understanding
heart

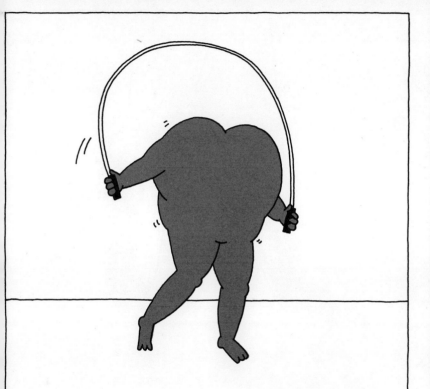

stout hearted

hearty support

affair of the heart

heart of darkness

heart of gold

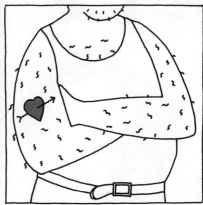

heart in the right place

chicken hearted

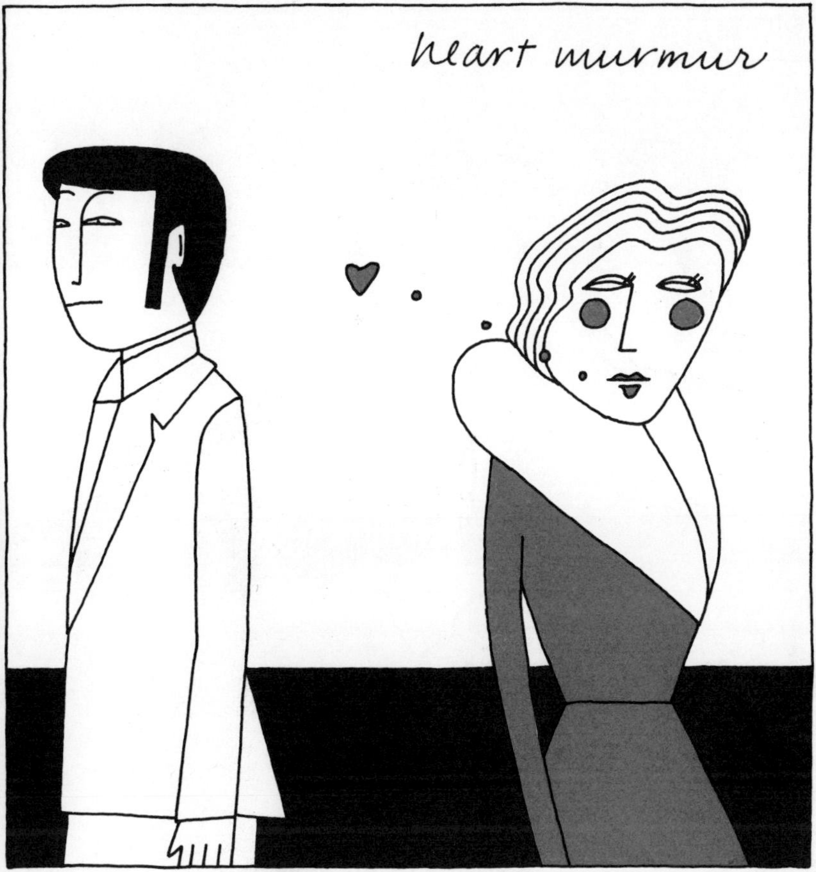
heart murmur

soft heart

foolish heart

heart donor

heartbeat

language of the heart

heart & soul

proud heart

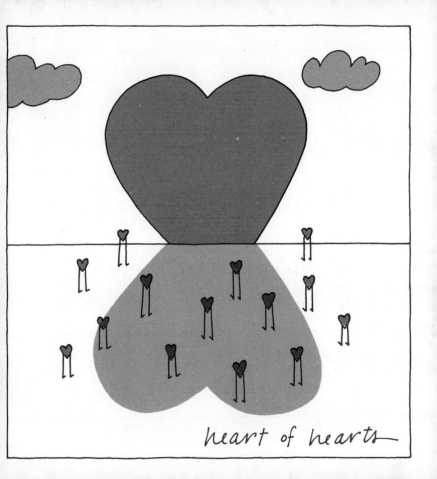

heart of hearts

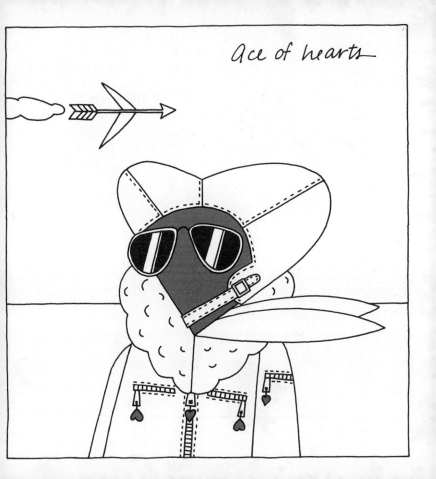

true heart/ artificial heart

the heart is a lonely hunter

cruel heart

listen to your heart

from the bottom of my heart

heart attack

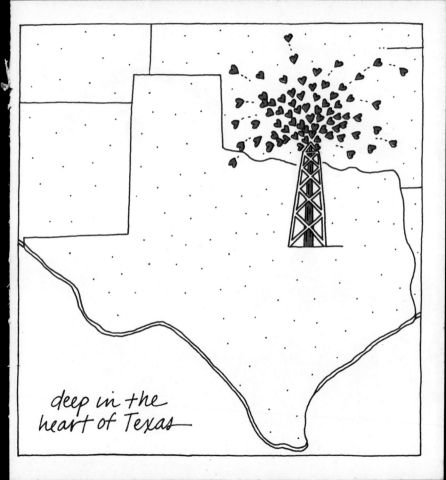

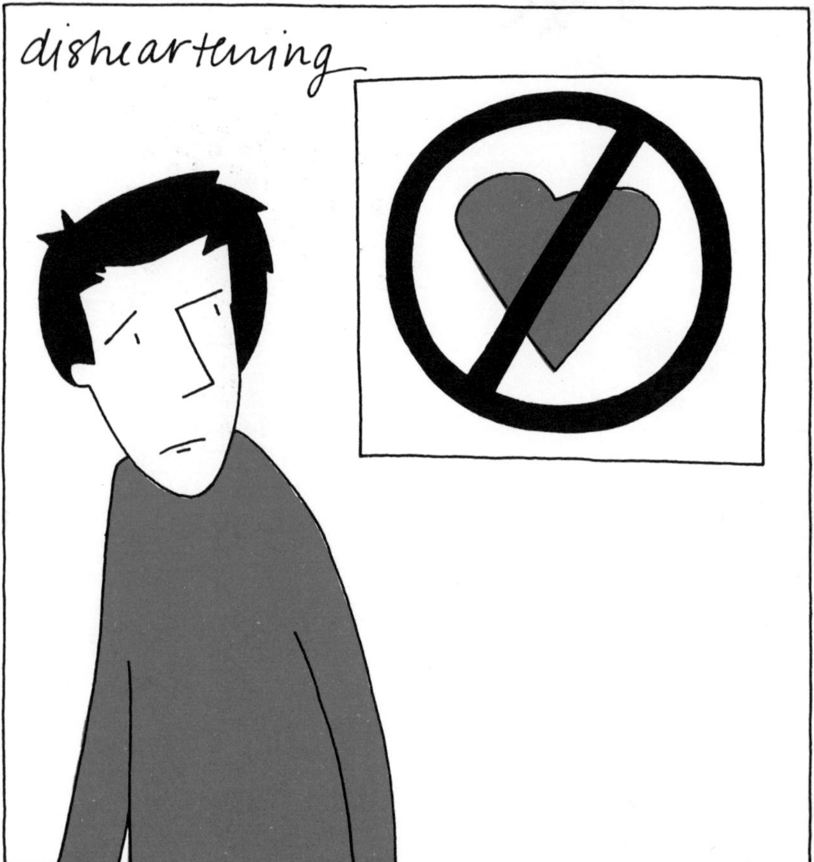
disheartening

heartwrenching

heart shaped square

heart shaped circle

heart shaped triangle

square shaped heart

heart shaped

heart of the financial district

the heart of Dixie

heart trouble

hearty laugh